NINE
HUMOROUS
TALES

NINE
HUMOROUS TALES

by

ANTON PAVLOVICH CHEKHOV

TRANSLATED BY

ISAAC GOLDBERG :: HENRY T. SCHNITTKIND

SECOND EDITION
(REVISED)

Short Story Index Reprint Series

BOOKS FOR LIBRARIES PRESS
PLAINVIEW, NEW YORK

19524

First Published 1918
Reprinted 1970

STANDARD BOOK NUMBER:
8369-3299-4

LIBRARY OF CONGRESS CATALOG CARD NUMBER:
76-106262

PRINTED IN THE UNITED STATES OF AMERICA

Anton Chekhov
(1860 - 1904)

AN IMPRESSION

IT may be more than mere accident that in the history of modern literature so many men of talent have turned from the practice of medicine to the profession of letters. The physician's office is largely a place of confession and his mind a focus gathering the light of human experiences from every angle. These, if he is a man of imagination as well as of science, he is prompted to reflect through the lens of fiction.

Though Anton Chekhov was a physician by training, (having been graduated from the Moscow University in 1884, at the age of twenty-four) he was a writer by preference. The wide knowledge gained from his medical studies and practice, coupled with the fact that his father was a peasant by birth and a city shop-keeper by occupation, must have contributed in great measure to the wide scope of his art.

American readers are by this time fairly well acquainted with Chekhov as a writer of many-sided interests and the possessor of a style that has been called the best since de Maupassant. One phase of the great Russian's work, however, has thus far been largely neglected; his humorous vein. This is all the more surprising because the Chekhov of the humorous tales naturally prompts comparison with our own O. Henry, although it would be unfair to both writers to extend the comparison too far.

Many of the tales of Chekhov, in their technique, resemble an unframed picture, the boundless wastes of the Russian steppe in miniature, while O. Henry's tales, on the other hand, at times contain more frame than picture,—the narrowness of the metropolis lined on either side by skyscrapers. Yet over skyscraper and steppe alike reposes that same heaven into which each in his own way has given us a glimpse.

Of the tales chosen for inclusion in this volume the first two resemble most closely the type of story generally associated in the public mind with the name of O. Henry. They are told with that same breeziness, that same crispness, and end with that same "punch" as characterize the American's work. The sad undercurrent of a story like "Her Gentleman Friend" is likewise not altogether foreign to our native writer. "Who Was She?" perhaps, is the most Maupassant-like story in the collection, while "Such Is Fame" strikes a note that is peculiar to the Russian himself. In stories like "The Scandal Monger," "Carelessness" and "Overspiced," Chekhov's humor seems to display a gentle humanity beneath the surface of the action; he is here not so much a deathless Puck who exclaims "Lord, what fools *these* mortals be!" as one of our very own who laughs "Lord, what fools *we* mortals be!" If Chekhov is more humanly self-revealing than de Maupassant, he is on the whole more deep than O. Henry. If O. Henry may be called the American Chekhov with a "punch," Chekhov may equally be termed the Russian O. Henry with a caress.

CONTENTS

A Work of Art

HOLDING under his arm an object wrapped in a newspaper, Sasha Smirnov, the only son of his mother, walked nervously into the office of Doctor Koshelkov. &1

"Well, my dear boy," exclaimed the doctor warmly, "how do you feel to-day? What's the good news?" &2

Sasha began to blink hesitantly, put his hand over his heart, and stammered nervously:

"My mother sends her regards and begs me to thank you.... I am my mother's only son, and you have saved my life.... You have cured me of a terrible disease and....and we both hardly know how to thank you."

"Come, come, my young friend, let us not speak of it," interrupted the doctor, literally melting with pleasure. "I have only done what anybody else in my place would have done."

"I am the only son of my mother.... We are poor people and consequently we are not in a position to pay you for your trouble....and it makes it very embarrassing for us, Doctor; although both of us, mother and I, who am the only son of my mother, beg of you to accept from us, as a token of our gratitude, this object which...is an object of rare worth, a wonderful masterpiece in antique bronze."

The doctor made a grimace.

"Why, my dear friend," he said, "it is entirely unnecessary. I don't need this in the least."

"Oh, no, no!" stammered Sasha. "I beg of you, please accept it!"

He began to unwrap the bundle, continuing his entreaties in the meantime:

"If you do not accept this, you will offend both my mother

11

and myself... This is a very rare work of art...an antique bronze. It is a relic left by my dead father. We have been prizing it as a very dear remembrance... My father used to buy up bronze antiques, selling them to lovers of old statuary... And now we continue in the same business, my mother and myself.''

Sasha undid the package and enthusiastically placed it on the table.

It was a low candelabrum of antique bronze, a work of real art representing a group: On a pedestal stood two figures of women clad in the costume of Mother Eve and in poses that I have neither the audacity nor the temperament to describe. These figures were smiling coquettishly and in general gave one the impression that, were it not for the fact that they were obliged to support the candle-stick, they would leap down from their pedestal and exhibit a performance which...my dear reader, I am even ashamed to think of it!

When the doctor espied the present, he slowly scratched his head, cleared his throat and blew his nose.

''Yes, indeed, a very pretty piece of work,'' he mumbled... ''But,—how shall I say it—not quite...I mean...rather unconventional...not a bit literary, is it?... You know...the devil knows...''

''Why?''

''Beelzebub himself could not have conceived anything more ugly. Should I place such a phantasmagoria upon my table I would pollute my entire home!''

''Why, Doctor, what a strange conception you have of art!'' cried Sasha in offended tones. ''This is a real masterpiece. Just look at it! Such is its harmonious beauty that just to contemplate it fills the soul with ecstasy and makes the throat choke down a sob! When you see such loveliness you forget all earthly things... Just look at it! What life, what motion, what expression!''

"I quite understand all this, my dear boy," interrupted the doctor. "But I am a married man. Little children run in and out of this room and ladies come here continually."

"Of course," said Sasha, "if you look at it through the eyes of the rabble, you see this noble masterpiece in an entirely different light. But you certainly are above all that, Doctor, and especially when your refusal to accept this gift will deeply offend both my mother and myself, who am the only son of my mother... You have saved my life...and in return we give you our dearest possession...and...my only regret is that we are unable to give you the mate to this candelabrum."

"Thanks, friend, many thanks... Remember me to your mother and... But for God's sake! You can see for yourself, can't you? Little children run in and out of this room, and ladies come here continually... However, leave it here! There's no use arguing with you."

"Don't say another word!" exclaimed Sasha joyously. "Put the candelabrum right here, next to the vase. By Jove, but it's a pity that I haven't got the mate to this to give you. But it can't be helped. Well, good-bye, Doctor!"

After the departure of Sasha the doctor looked for a long time at the candelabrum and scratched his head.

"This is beautiful, all right," he thought. "It would be a pity to throw it away... And yet I dare not keep it... Hm!... Now who in the world is there to whom I can present or donate it?"

After long deliberation he hit upon a good friend of his, the lawyer Ukhov, to whom he was indebted for legal services.

"Fine!" chuckled the doctor. "Being such a close friend of his, I cannot very well offer him money, and so I will give him this piece of indecency instead... And he's just the man for it...single, and somewhat of a gay bird, too."

No sooner thought than done. Dressing himself, the doctor took the candelabrum and went to the home of Ukhov.

"Good morning, old chap!" he said. "I have come here to thank you for your trouble...You will not take money, and I will therefore repay you by presenting you with this exquisite masterpiece... Now say for yourself, isn't it a dream?"

As soon as the lawyer caught sight of it he was exhilarated with its beauty.

"What a wonderful work of art!" he laughed uproariously. "Ye gods, what conceptions artists will get into their heads! What alluring charm! Where did you get this little dandy?"

But now his exhilaration had oozed away and he became frightened. Looking stealthily toward the door, he said:

"But, I can't accept it, old chap. You must take it right back."

"Why?" asked the doctor in alarm.

"Because...because...my mother often visits me, my clients come here...and besides, I would be disgraced even in the eyes of my servants."

"Don't say another word!" cried the doctor gesticulating wildly. "You simply have got to accept it! It would be rank ingratitude for you to refuse it! Such a masterpiece! What motion, what expression... You will greatly offend me if you don't take it!"

"If only this were daubed over or covered with fig-leaves..."

But the doctor refused to listen to him. Gesticulating even more wildly, he ran out of Ukhov's house, happy in the thought that he was rid of the present.

When the doctor was gone the lawyer carefully examined the candelabrum, and then, just as the doctor had done, he began to wonder what in the world he could do with it.

"A very beautiful object," he thought. "It is a pity to throw it away, and yet it is disgraceful to keep it. I had best present it to someone... I've got it!... This very evening I'm going to give it to the comedian Shoshkin. The rascal loves such things, and besides, this is his benefit night..."

No sooner thought than done. That afternoon the well-packed candelabrum was brought to the comedian Shoshkin.

That whole evening the dressing-room of the comedian Shoshkin was besieged by men who hastened to inspect the present. And during all that time the room reechoed with hilarious laughter which most closely resembled the neighing of horses.

If any of the actresses approached the door and said, "May I enter?" the hoarse voice of Shoshkin was immediately heard to reply:

"Oh, no, no, my darling, you mustn't! I am not dressed!"

After the performance the comedian shrugged his shoulders, gesticulated with his hands and said:

"Now what in the world am I to do with this? I live in a private apartment! I am often visited by actresses! And this isn't a photograph that one could conceal in a drawer!"

"Why don't you sell it?" suggested the wig maker "There is a certain old woman who buys up antique bronzes... Her name is Smirnova... You had better take a run over there; they'll show you the place all right, everybody knows her..."

The comedian followed his advice...

Two days later Koshelkov, his head supported on his hand, was sitting in his office and concocting pills. Suddenly the door was opened and into the office rushed Sasha. He was smiling radiantly and his breast heaved with joy... In his hands he held something wrapped in a newspaper.

"Doctor!" he cried breathlessly. "Imagine my joy! As luck would have it, I've just succeeded in getting the mate to your candelabrum! Mother is so happy! I am the only son of my mother... You have saved my life..."

And Sasha, quivering with thankfulness and rapture, placed a candelabrum before the doctor. The latter opened his mouth, as if about to say something, but uttered not a word... His power of speech was gone...

Vengeance

LYEV Savvitch Turmanov, a worthy citizen who possessed a nice little fortune, a nice little wife, and a nice little bald spot on his head, was celebrating the birthday of one of his friends with a game of cards. After a strenuous effort which covered his forehead with perspiration, he suddenly recollected that he and the bottle had been strangers for quite a long time.

He rose and, balancing himself on his tiptoes between the tables, went into the guest room where the youngsters were dancing. Here he smiled graciously and with a fatherly caress he patted the shoulders of a young skinny druggist, slipping forthwith through a little door which led into the dining room. On a little round table in this room stood bottles and glasses with whiskey... Among other refreshments he spied a plate containing half a herring alluringly decorated with onions and parsley.

Lyev Savvitch filled a glass, made a gesture as though about to deliver a speech, emptied the glass and made a wry face. Then he jabbed the herring with the fork and. . . . But suddenly he overheard voices behind the wall.

"Very well," spoke a woman's voice, "but when?"

"My wife," said Lyev Savvitch to himself, recognizing the voice. "I wonder whom she is talking to?"

"Whenever you desire," replied a deep and heavy bass.

"Today it is not convenient, tomorrow I shall be busy the whole day. . ."

"This is Dentjarev," thought Lyev recognizing the bass voice of his friend. "Et tu, Brute! And so she has caught you, too, in her net? By Jove, nothing seems to satisfy her. I've never seen such a restless woman in my life! Not a single day can she live through without her little romance!"

"Yes, tomorrow I shall be busy," continued the heavy bass. "What do you say to writing me a little note? That will give me great pleasure. . . But we must introduce some system into our correspondence. Let's see if we can't find some way. It isn't a bit safe to send our letters through the mail. Your turkey is liable to intercept our correspondence in that way. And when you write to me, my wife might sometimes open the letter in my absence, and then!..."

"What shall we do, then?"

"We've got to find some way, It won't do to send them through a servant, for your lobster of a husband is surely watching the servants... I wonder whether he's still at that game of cards?"

"Yes, and he always loses, too, the big boob!"

"He must be lucky in love, then," laughed Dentjarev. . . "Now, listen, my little girlie. I've hit upon a plan. On my way from the office tomorrow at six o'clock I pass by the Public Garden where I am to meet the Inspector. And so, sweetheart, I want you to manage just a little before six, but not later, to place a note for me in the marble vase that stands to the left of the grape-vine arbor. Do you know the place I mean?"

"Certainly I do."

"That will be poetical and mysterious and unique. And in this way neither your wooden-headed meal ticket nor my old shrew will know anything about it. Do you understand?"

Lyev Savvitch emptied another glass and returned to the game. The discovery which he had just made did not surprise him; it did not even arouse his jealousy or anger. He had long outgrown the habit of scolding and fuming and raging and even occasionally beating his wife for her misbehavior. He had long ago given up all hope and nowadays he merely looked through his fingers at his wife's romantic vagaries. And yet he was now feeling uncomfortable. His pride and self-love were touched to the quick at such appelations as "boob," "lobster," and "wooden-headed meal ticket."

"Ye gods, what a blackguard this Dentjarev is!" he thought as he marked down his score. When he meets me in the street he pretends to be a good friend, grinning and patting me in the belly; and yet see what he can do behind my back. When he speaks to me man to man, I'm his friend, and when he talks behind my back, lo and behold! I'm a boob and a lobster. . ."

And the more he lost at the game, the more indignant he felt.

"Why, his mother's milk is still wet on his lips," he thought, crushing in his rage the piece of chalk which he held. "He's nothing but a little snipe. . . If it were not for the fact that I wouldn't condescend to slap his face, I'd show him what a wooden-headed meal ticket can do!"

At supper he was unable to look Dentjarev straight in the face, although the latter seemed as if on purpose determined to annoy him with his questions. Had he won or lost? Why was he so sad? and so forth. He even had the nerve to scold Lyev's wife for not being sufficiently careful of her husband's health. . . And his wife, as though nothing had happened, looked at her husband with dove's eyes, chatting so innocently and laughing so genuinely that the devil himself could not have accused her of faithlessness.

And when he came home, Lyev Savvitch felt angry and dissatisfied, as though he had eaten old rubbers instead of veal for supper. He might have made an effort to forget the whole incident were it not for his wife's laughter and prattle which reminded him every minute of the boob, the lobster, the wooden-headed meal ticket.

"I should have punched him in the jaw, that low life," he thought. "Right in front of everybody. . ."

And he pictured to himself how nice it would be to thrash Dentjarev, or to challenge him and shoot him like a bird. . . It wouldn't be a bad idea to make him lose his job. . . Or perhaps it would be best to put some disgusting object into the marble vase, something with a nasty smell, — a dead rat for instance. . . Perhaps he might abscond his wife's letter and put in its place a silly poem signed "Your Akulyka," or something else of that sort.

For a long time he paced through his bed-room cooling his rage with these reveries. Suddenly he stopped and slapped his forehead.

"Hooray, I've got it!" he exclaimed, beaming with joy. "This is a wonderful idea! Excellent!"

When his wife fell asleep, he sat down near the table and after long deliberation, disguising his handwriting and purposely committing a number of errors, he penned the following:

"To the Merchant Dulinov.

Dere Sir:—

If up to six oclock dis evenin, the twelvth of September, you fale to put two hundred dollars inter the marble vaze wich is situaited in the Public Garden, just to the left of the graip-vine arber, you will be a dead man and your dry-gudes store will be blown up."

And signing this missive, Lyev Savvitch jumped up enthusiastically.

"Isn't this a wonderful plan?" he growled rubbing his hands together. "Immense, even if I do say so myself! Beelzebub himself couldn't have hit upon a happier idea! It is quite certain that the store-keeper Dulinov will get so scared that he will immediately notify the police. And they will surely send a number of detectives who will hide themselves among the bushes and watch. . . At six o'clock, when Dentjarev comes for his letter, they will nab the poor bloke,—and by Jove, won't he get pepper to smell!. . . He'll be scared blue, and before everything is cleared up, the rascal will get a good chance to cool his amorous ardor in jail. . . And it will serve him right, too. . . Bravo, Lyev Savvitch!. . ."

He put a stamp on the envelope and going down stairs deposited it himself in the letter box.

He fell asleep with a radiant smile playing upon his lips. For many a long night had he not slept so sweetly and so soundly.

When he awoke in the morning and recalled his plan he felt so happy that he actually began to purr and even went so far as to flirt with his faithless wife. . .

On his way to work and later, while sitting in his office, he kept smiling to himself as he pictured Dentjarev's terror on finding himself caught in the trap. . .

Toward six o'clock he could restrain himself no longer and ran to the Public Garden in order to witness with his own eyes the downfall of his enemy.

"Aha!" he thought, seeing a policeman in the vicinity.

Arriving at the well-known arbor he sat down behind a tree and, fixing his sharp, stern eyes upon the vase, awaited the arrival of Dentjarev. He sat as if on pins and needles in his impatience.

Precisely at six Dentjarev appeared. The young man was evidently in a very good humor. His silk hat encircled his head at a coquettish angle, and through his unbuttoned coat his very soul seemed to glitter together with his vest. He was smoking a cigar and whistling a merry tune. . .

"Now, you big slob, I'll show you who is a lobster and a wooden-headed meal ticket!" chuckled Turmanov. "You just wait!"

Dentjarev approached the vase and languidly put his hand into it. . . Lyev Savvitch half rose and fixed his eyes upon him. . . The young man took a tiny package out of the vase, carefully examined it on all sides and shrugged his shoulders. Then he undid the package, shrugged his shoulders again and opened his mouth in astonishment; the package contained two brand new one hundred dollar bills. . .

Dentjarev looked long at these bills. Finally, shrugging his shoulders once more, he put them into his pocket and said, "Many thanks!"

Poor Lyev Savvitch heard these words "many thanks." That entire evening he stood opposite Dulinov's dry-goods store, shook his fist at the sign and raged:

"You coward! You soul of a penny store-keeper! Pinhead! Ass! You pot-bellied rabbit you! . . ."

Her Gentleman Friend

CHARMING Vanda, or, as she was named in her passport, the honorable citizeness Nastasia Kanavkina, found herself, upon her discharge from the hospital, in a position worse than any she had ever known: without lodgings and without a kopek. What was to be done?

Her first thought was the pawnshop. Thither she went, pawning her turquoise ring, the one "valuable" she possessed. For the ring she received a rouble. But...what can a ruble buy? For such a sum one can purchase neither an up-to-date short jacket, nor a picture hat, nor gold-colored slippers; and without these articles she felt just as though she were naked. It seemed to her that not only the people she passed, but even the horses and the dogs stared at her and poked fun at the simplicity of her clothes. She thought only of her toilet, while the matter of food and shelter gave her not the slightest concern.

"If I should only meet a gentleman friend," she thought. "I'd ask him for a small loan... Nobody would refuse me, for..."

But no gentleman friends came her way. It would not have been difficult to find some that evening at the "Renaissance," but they surely would not admit her into the "Renaissance" in her plain garb and without a hat. What was she to do?

After long hesitation, when she had wearied of walking, sitting and meditating, Vanda resolved to try the last recourse: to walk right into the apartment of one of her men friends and ask him for money.

"But whom shall I go to?" she debated. "Not to Misha... that wouldn't do—he's married and has a family... And the red-headed old fellow is at his office now..."

The dentist Finkel came to her mind. He was a converted

Jew, who, three months before, had presented her with a brace-let; once at a supper in the "German club," she had poured a glass of beer over his pate. At thought of this Finkel, Vanda was seized with frightful delight.

"He'll certainly give me something if I only find him at home..." she thought, on the way to the dentist. "If he doesn't, I'll smash all his lamps for him..."

By the time she had reached the doctor's door her plan was fully formulated: she would run up the steps with laughter, burst into the dentist's private office and request twenty-five roubles... But when she stretched her hand toward the bell the plan vanished into thin air, as if by magic: Vanda was sud-denly seized with fright,—something that had never happened to her. She had been bold and impudent, only in tipsy company; but now, in common clothes, in the role of an ordinary beggar who was not even presentable, she felt embarrassed and low-spirited. Shame and fear overwhelmed her.

"Perhaps he has already forgotten me..." she thought, while she summoned the courage to pull the bell. "And how can I approach him in this garb? Like a beggar or some shabby shop-girl...."

And hesitantly she pulled the bell.

Behind the door sounded footsteps; it was the doorkeeper.

"Is the doctor in?" she asked.

Now she would have felt far better if the doorkeeper should answer "No." But instead of a reply he simply led her into the vestibule and helped her remove her coat.

The staircase seemed wonderfully luxurious to her, but of all this luxury her eye was first struck by a tall mirror in which she beheld a disgraceful object without an up-to-date jacket, without a picture hat and without gold-colored slippers. And it seemed strange to Vanda that, now that she was so poorly clad and looked like a seamstress or a washerwoman, she was again seized

with a feeling of shame; she possessed none of her former bold-
ness or insolence and even to herself she was no longer Vanda,
but, as of yore, Nastya Kanavkina...

"Please step this way," said the chambermaid, leading her
into the office. "The doctor will be in directly... Be seated."

Vanda sank into a soft armchair.

"I'll just say to him: Lend me the money," she thought.
"That's certainly proper, for he knows me. If only that maid
would leave the room! With her around it would be very hard...
And why on earth does she stand here, of all places?"

After about five minutes the door opened and Finkel, tall,
dark, with fat cheeks and bulging eyes, stepped in. His cheeks,
his paunch, his broad hips—everything about him was com-
placent and repulsive. At the "Renaissance" and at the "German club" he was usually tipsy, spent a good deal on women
and bore their pranks patiently. For instance, when Vanda had
poured a glass of beer over his head, he had merely smiled and
shaken his finger at her. Now, however, he appeared bloated
and sleepy; he looked into the room with an air of importance
and superiority, and was chewing something.

"What can I do for you?" he asked, without looking at her.

Vanda cast a glance at the grave countenance of the maid, then
at the over-fed figure of Finkel, who plainly seemed not to recognize her, and then—she blushed...

"What can I do for you?" repeated the dentist, now somewhat irritated.

"I've got a tooth-ache..." stammered Vanda.

"Aha... Which tooth? Where?"

Vanda suddenly recalled that she had a cavity.

"At the right, my lower jaw..." she said.

"H'm! Open your mouth."

Finkel furrowed his forehead, held his breath and began to
examine the aching tooth.

"Does it hurt?" he asked, poking about in her tooth with a sharp instrument.

"Yes..." lied Vanda. "Shall I remind him?" she thought. "He would certainly recognize me then... But...the maid! What is she standing there for?"

Finkel suddenly began to puff like a steam-engine straight into her mouth, and said, "I should advise you not to fill it... This tooth will be of no use to you anyway."

After he had dug about the tooth for a few moments more and had soiled Vanda's lips and gums with his tobacco-stained fingers, he again held his breath and shoved something cold into her mouth...

Suddenly Vanda felt a terrible pain, let out a shriek and seized Finkel by the arm.

"All right, never mind," he murmured. "Don't be so timid. You would have had little use from this tooth, anyway. One must be brave."

And his tobacco-stained fingers, covered with blood, held before her eyes the extracted tooth, while the maid stepped forward and brought her a bowl.

"When you get home, rinse your mouth with cold water..." said Finkel, "and the bleeding will stop."

He stood before her in the attitude of a man who is waiting impatiently to be rid of his visitor and to be left alone.

"Good-by..." she said, turning to the door.

"H'm!... And who is to pay me for my services?" asked Finkel in a merry voice.

"Oh...yes..." gasped Vanda, suddenly recalling herself. She blushed and handed the dentist the rouble she had received for her turquoise ring.

Stepping into the street she felt a keener sense of shame than before; but she was no longer ashamed of her poverty. She no longer was conscious that she lacked a picture hat and an up-to-date jacket. She walked along the street expectorating blood, and every spot of blood spoke to her of her life, of her evil, bitter life, and of the insults that she had experienced,—and those she would have to endure to-morrow, and next week, and next year—and all her life until death.

"Oh, how terrible!" she whispered. "My God, how terrible!"

But on the next day she was at the "Renaissance," dancing there. She was dressed in a huge, red hat, an up-to-date jacket and gold-colored slippers. And she was treated to supper by a young merchant from Kazan.

Who Was She?

"**D**O tell us a story, Pyotr Ivanovitch!" begged the young ladies.

The colonel stroked his gray side-whiskers, cleared his throat and began:

"It happened in the year 1843, when our regiment was stationed before Chenstokhov. That winter, my dear ladies, was an exceedingly severe one, so that not a day passed without the sentries having their noses frozen or the streets being piled high with snow. The intense cold weather began in October and lasted into April. In those days, I must tell you, I didn't look so old and passé as now; on the contrary, I was—as you may well imagine—a dashing fellow, in the full bloom of youth; in a word, a handsome young man. I used to strut about like a peacock, threw money right and left and twirled my side-whiskers unlike any other lieutenant on earth. Yes... I needed merely to wink an eye, clank my spurs and twirl my whiskers, and the proudest beauty would be transformed into an obedient lambkin. I had a sweet-tooth for women, just like a spider's for a fly, and if I were to count for you, my dear ladies, the number of Polish and Jewish women that languished for me in those days, then I assure you that there would not be enough figures in Mathematics for the reckoning...

"And kindly remember that I was regimental aide-de-camp, that I danced the mazurka excellently, and was married to a most charming woman, Heaven rest her soul! You simply cannot imagine what a dare-devil rogue I was. Why, whenever in our district any love catastrophe occurred, such as a Jew having his temple-locks torn off, or a Pole being boxed in the ears, they knew at once that second-lieutenant Vivertov had done it.

27

"As aide-de-camp it was my duty to journey about the district quite frequently. Now I'd be off to purchase oats or hay, now to sell to the Jews or the Poles horses that had outlived their usefulness to the army. But most often, dear ladies, under the pretext of duty I would ride away to a rendezvous with some woman, or to wealthy landowners, for a game of cards...

"One Christmas eve,—I remember it as clearly as if it happened only yesterday—I was journeying from Chenstokhov to the village of Shevelki, whither I had been sent on official business. The weather, I must tell you, was murderous... The cold was so bitter and biting that even the horses could scarcely endure it and I and my driver, within half an hour, were human icicles... If the cold had been all, we might have found means to cope with it, but on the middle of the way there suddenly broke out a snowstorm. Eddies of snow whirled and danced about us like a troop of devils. The wind raged as if his wife had been stolen; the road disappeared... In less than ten minutes I, the driver and the horses were completely covered with snow.

" 'Your excellency, we have lost the way,' announced the driver.

" 'The deuce! Why didn't you keep your eyes open? Well, keep right on. Perhaps we'll come to some human habitation!'

"Well, we rode and rode, and turned and turned, and thus toward midnight our horses stumbled upon the gate of an estate that belonged, if I remember correctly, to Count Boyadlovski, a wealthy Polish nobleman. Poles and Jews are one and the same to me, like mustard after dinner, but they're a hospitable lot, — you've got to concede that to them, and when it comes to passionate women, none can equal the Poles...

"We were admitted ... Count Boyadlovski himself, at that time, was living at Paris, and we were received by his steward Kasimir Khapzinski, likewise a Pole. I recall that before an hour had passed I was seated in the steward's home, flirting with his wife, drinking and playing cards. After I had won five ducats and more than extinguished my thirst I asked to be shown to my chamber. Since there was no more room in the steward's house, I was led to a chamber in the Count's dwelling.

" 'Aren't you afraid of ghosts?' asked the steward, leading me into a medium-sized room, which was next to a vast empty hall, cold and dark.

" 'Is this a haunted house, then?' I asked, while I heard the hollow echo repeat my words and my footsteps.

" 'I don't know!' " laughed the Pole. " 'But it seems to me that this place is an ideal one for ghosts and spirits.' "

"I had poured down a goodly quantity behind my belt, and was as soused as forty-thousand cobblers; but, to tell the truth, at these words I felt icy shivers run down my spine. Devil take it! Rather a hundred Circassians than one ghost! But there was no help for it. I undressed and went to bed . . . My candle barely illumined the walls, upon which there hung ancestral portraits, one more frightful than the other, — ancient weapons, hunting horns and like things . . . The stillness of the grave reigned in the room, and only in the adjacent hall could be heard the scampering of the mice, and their gnawing at the old furniture. Outside, however, raged a hellish din . . . The wind sang a funeral mass, the trees bent, groaning and weeping; some devilish object, probably a shutter, squeaked lugubriously and struck against the window-frame. Add to this that my head was whirling round and round, and with it the whole world . . . When I closed my eyes it seemed to me that my bed was flying through the whole house, playing chase with the spirits. In order to lessen my fears, first of all I extinguished the candle, for empty rooms seem much more horrible when lighted than in the darkness. . ."

The three young ladies who were listening to the Colonel edged closer to the speaker and gazed at him in motionless expectancy.

"Well," continued the Colonel, "as hard as I tried to fall asleep, I simply could not. Now it seemed to me that thieves were climbing in over the window-sill, now I heard somewhere a mysterious whispering, and now somebody touched me on the shoulder—everything seemed to me the work of diabolical hands,—a mood known to all who have ever been in a condition of nervous tension. Yet, can you imagine it, — through all this devilish clatter and chaos of sounds I suddenly distinguish·a noise that resembles the gliding of slippers. I listen intently and hear — what do you think? — somebody approaching my door. There is a cough; the door is opened.

" 'Who is there?' " I ask, rising.

" 'It is I . . . have no fear!' answered a woman's voice.

"I went to the door . . . Several seconds passed and I felt two hands, soft as eiderdown, placed upon my shoulders."

" 'I love you. . . You are dearer to me than life itself,' spoke the melodious voice of a woman.

"A hot breath scorched my cheek... I forgot the snowstorm, the ghosts, — everything in the world, and wound my arm around her waist . . . and such a waist! Such waists nature can make only for special orders, and even then, only once in ten years. . . Thin, as if chiseled; hot, ephemeral as the breath of a child! I could no longer restrain myself and clasped her in my arms. . . Our lips met in a long, passionate kiss and . . . I swear it, by all the women in the world, I'll carry the memory of that kiss with me to the grave.—"

The Colonel was silent, swallowed a half glass of water and with a lowered voice, continued:

"—The next morning, when I looked out of the window, I saw that the snowstorm had increased in violence. . . It was impossible to proceed on my journey. So I had to remain at the steward's all day long, playing cards and drinking. At night I found myself again in the empty house, and exactly at midnight I embraced the selfsame waist as the night before. . .

"Yes, dear ladies, had it not been for love I should have died of ennui that time, or else surrendered completely to Bacchus.—"

The Colonel sighed, arose and began to pace silently up and down the salon.

"Well. . . and what happened after that?" asked one of the young ladies, who was dying of curiosity.

"Nothing. The next day I was again on my journey."

"Yes. . .but who was this woman?" the young ladies asked, bashfully.

"Why, that's very evident, isn't it?"

"Not at all!"

"It was my wife!"

The three young ladies sprang to their feet as if they had been stung by a tarantula.

"Yes. . . but how do you explain it?" they asked.

"Heavens! What is there about this that is so difficult to understand?" asked the Colonel, shrugging his shoulders with vexation. "I expressed myself clearly enough, I believe! I was riding to Shevelki with my wife . . . She spent the night in the empty house, in the room next to mine. . . Isn't that simple enough?"

"Mmm. . ." murmured the young ladies, dropping their hands into their laps, disappointed. "You began so well, and ended Lord knows how. . . Only your wife!. . Pardon us, but the tale isn't a bit interesting and. . . not at all clever."

"Now, that's comical! You'd prefer it to be not my lawfully wedded wife, but some strange woman! Ah, my dear ladies, my dear ladies! If that's how you are now, how will you be when you are married?"

The young ladies were embarrassed, and made no reply.

"No. It's altogether. . . unbecoming!" exploded one of them, unable to restrain herself any longer. "Why did you need to tell us the tale if it had such an end? There's nothing nice in the story. . . or exceptional, either!''

"You began so entrancingly and then, all of a sudden. . ." added her companion. "You were merely poking fun at us. . ."

"Well, well, well. . . it was only a joke on my part. . ." said the Colonel. "Please don't be angry, dear ladies, "I was only jesting. It was not my wife, but the steward's. . ."

"Yes?"

The young ladies suddenly recovered their joyful spirits; their eyes sparkled. . . They edged closer to the Colonel, poured out wine for him and showered him with questions. Their ennui disappeared. And the supper soon disappeared with it, for the young ladies attacked the meal with ravenous appetite.

The Scandal Monger

A KHINEYEV, the teacher of penmanship, was marrying off his daughter Natalia to Loshadinikh, the instructor in geography and history.

The wedding festivities were in full swing. The hall resounded with singing, playing and the scuffle of dancing feet. Hired servants in black frock coats and dirty white cravats were scurrying madly about the room. Tarantulov, the instructor in mathematics, the Frenchman Pasdequoi and Msda, the junior inspector were seated together upon the sofa telling the guests, amidst many interruptions and corrections of each other, all the cases known to them of persons having been buried alive, and were moreover airing their views upon spiritualism. None of the three believed in spiritualism, to be sure, but they were willing to admit that there was much in this world that could not be explained by human intelligence.

In another room Dodonski, teacher of literature, was explaining the circumstances under which a sentry might fire upon civilians. The conversation was, as you see, a trifle gruesome, yet highly animated.

Through the windows, from without, looked in a crowd of envious people whose social position did not grant them the privilege of entrance.

At exactly twelve o'clock the master of the house, Akhineyev, stepped into the kitchen to see whether all was ready for the wedding supper. From floor to ceiling the kitchen steamed with an aroma of geese, ducks and countless other appetizing dishes. Upon two tables were beheld, in artistic disorder, the ingredients of a truly Lucullian banquet. And Marfa the cook, a buxom woman with a two-story stomach, was busy about the table.

"My dear woman, just let me have a look at that fish," requested Akhineyev, chuckling and rubbing his palms together. "Mm! What a delicious odor! Enough to make you eat the whole kitchen up! Let's see that fish, do!"

Marfa went over to one of the chairs and carefully removed a greasy newspaper, underneath which there reposed upon a gigantic platter a huge whitefish, garnished with capers, olives and vegetables. Akhineyev looked at the fish and almost melted with rapture. His countenance beamed; his eyes almost popped out of their sockets. He leaned forward and with his lips made a sound resembling the squeal of an ungreased axle. For a moment he stood motionless, then snapped his fingers and smacked his lips again.

"Aha! The music of a passionate kiss... Whom are you kissing there?...Marfa?" came a voice from the adjoining room, and in the doorway there appeared the close-cropped head of Akhineyev's colleague Vanykin.

"Who is the lucky fellow? Aha. . . . fine! Mr. Akhineyev himself! Bravo, grandpa! Excellent! A nice little tête-a-tête with a charming lady. . ."

"I'm not kissing anybody," retorted Akhineyev, embarrassed. "What an idea! You. . . I was merely smacking my lips. . . with delight. . . as I looked upon the fish here. . ."

Vanykin's features wrinkled with laughter and he disappeared. Akhineyev turned red.

"The deuce!" he thought. "Now this fellow is going around everywhere gossiping about me. A thing like this can easily spread through the whole city. . . The jackass!"

Akhineyev returned to the hall shyly, and glanced furtively in all directions for Vanykin. That worthy was standing by the piano telling something in his most cavalier-like manner to the inspector's mother-in-law, who smiled in evident pleasure.

"It's about me!" suspected Akhineyev. "About me, devil take the rascal! And she, she believes every word and laughs!

Such a silly goose! Good God! No, I must not allow this. No...
I must do something to discredit him in advance... I'll speak to
everybody about the incident and unmask him as a stupid gossip-
monger!"

Akhineyev scratched himself and then, still in embarrass-
ment, walked over to Pasdequoi.

"I was just in the kitchen to settle some details about the
supper," he said to the Frenchman. "I know that you're very
fond of fish, and I've got one down there about two yards long!
He-he-he!... Yes, and then, — I almost forgot it — In the
kitchen just now, such a funny joke! You see, I come into the
kitchen and want to take a look at the dishes... I see the fish and
from sheer delight... such a splendid specimen... I smacked my
lips, so... And at this very moment in pops that bad sheep Vanykin and says... ha-ha-ha!... and says, 'Aha! You're kissing
somebody here?'... Such a fool, — imagining that I was kissing
Marfa, the cook! Why, that woman looks as if...—Fie! To kiss
a thing like her! There's a fool for you! Such an ass!"

"Who's that?" asked Tarantulov, coming in.

"Vanykin! You see, I come into the kitchen..."

The tale of Marfa and the fish was repeated.

"Think of it! Why, I'd just as soon kiss a mongrel as kiss
Marfa..." And Akhineyev, turning around, noticed Mr. Msda.

"We were just speaking of Vanykin," said Akhineyev to
Msda. "Such a simpleton! Pops into the kitchen, sees me near
Marfa the cook and at once makes up a whole story. 'So, you're
kissing Marfa?' says he to me. He was a little bit tipsy, upon my
word! And I answered that I'd sooner kiss a turkey than kiss
Marfa. And I reminded him, too, that I was a married man.
Think of his silly idea! Ridiculous!"

"What's ridiculous?" asked the rector, happening to pass
by.

"That chap Vanykin. I'm in the kitchen, you understand,
looking at the fish..."

And so forth. In the course of a half hour nearly all the guests were fully informed of the story of the fish.

"Now let him tell as many people as he wishes!" thought Akhineyev, rubbing his palms. "Just let him! As soon as he begins I can say to him, 'Spare your breath, dear friend! We know all about it already!'"

And the thought so comforted Akhineyev that he drank four glasses more than were good for him. After the supper he led the newlywed couple to the bridal chamber, went to bed and slept like a log. By the next morning he had forgotten the tale of the fish completely. But woe! Man proposes and God disposes... The evil tongue accomplished its wicked work and Akhineyev's cunning was all in vain! Exactly a week later, on a Wednesday, just after the third lesson had begun and Akhineyev was standing in the class-room correcting the exaggerated slope of the pupil Vissekin's handwriting, the Director stepped over to him and called him to one side.

"My dear Mr. Akhineyev," said the Director. — "You will pardon me. . . It is really none of my business, but I must speak to you about it. . . It is my official duty. . . You must know that the rumor is running through the city that you have certain relations with. . . with your cook. . . Of course it's no affair of mine, as I have said, but. . . live with her, kiss her. . . to your heart's content. But I beg of you, not so publicly! I beg of you! Do not forget your high calling!"

A cold shiver ran down Akhineyev's spine and he lost his self-composure. As if he had been stung by a gigantic swarm of bees, or scalded with boiling water, he flew to his home. On the way it seemed to him that the whole city were staring at him as if he had been tarred and feathered... At home a new vexation was awaiting him.

"Why don't you eat?" asked his wife at dinner time. "What are you dreaming about? Your love? Are you yearning for Marfa? You Mohammedan, you! I know everything! My eyes have been opened! You... barbarian!"

And slap! he received a blow over the cheek. He arose from the table and as if in a trance, with neither hat nor coat, he went to Vanykin. He found Vanykin at home.

"You slanderer!" cried Akhineyev, turning upon him. "Why have you soiled my reputation before the whole world? How dare you have slandered me!"

"What do you mean, — 'slandered?' Where did you ever get that notion?"

"Then who *did* invent the story that I had been kissing Marfa? I suppose it wasn't you, eh? Not you, eh?"

Vanykin began to blink, and his whole lively countenance was convulsed with twitching. Raising his eyes to the ikon in the corner, he cried out, "May God punish me! I swear by the salvation of my soul that I never repeated a word of the story! May I be cursed with eternal damnation! May I..."

There was no questioning Vanykin's sincerity. It was clear that he had not spread the gossip.

"But who then? Who?" muttered Akhineyev, beating his fists against his breasts and mentally going over the list of all his friends. "Who then?"

Carelessness

PYOTR Petrovitch Strizhin, the same whose rubbers had been stolen last year, was returning home from a Christening party at two o'clock in the morning.

In order not to arouse the household he quietly undressed in the hall and breathlessly tiptoed into his bedroom, where, without turning on a light, he was about to lie down.

Strizhin was a fellow with the face of a fool, living a regular and sober life and reading only books with a moral purpose. It was only on such a festive occasion as the present that, in honor of the newly born child of Lyubov Spirodovna, he allowed himself to empty four glasses of whiskey and a glass of wine which tasted like castor-oil. These hot beverages are like sea-water or fame: the more you quaff, the more thirsty you become. . .

And now, while he was undressing, Strizhin suddenly acquired an overwhelming thirst.

"If I'm not mistaken," said he, "there is a bottle of whiskey in Dashenka's cupboard. It's right there in the corner, if I'm not mistaken. . . She'll never notice the difference if I take only a little glass."

After a short deliberation he mastered his timidity and went to the cupboard.

Opening the door of the cupboard slowly, he found a bottle in the right-hand corner. He filled a glass in the dark, replaced the bottle, crossed himself, and swallowed the contents with a single gulp.

And here something remarkable happened. A terrible force, like a bomb, hurled Strizhin from the cupboard to the trunk. His eyes beheld a flash of lightning, he began to choke and shiver as though he had just fallen into a swamp full of blood-suckers. It seemed to him that instead of whiskey he had just swallowed a piece of dynamite which blew him to pieces and scattered his head, his arms, his legs, the house and the entire street in all directions, way up in the air, the devil knows whither. . .

For about three minutes he lay motionless and breathless on the trunk. Then he rose and asked himself:

"Where am I?"

When he came to himself, he smelt for the first time a strong odor of kerosene.

"Holy Father in Heaven!" he cried, I've drunk kerosene instead of whiskey! And a shudder passed through his body.

The thought that he had poisoned himself threw him into an ague. And that he really had poisoned himself was evident not only from the odor in the room, but also from the sparks that danced before his eyes, from the ringing in his ears and from the stabbing pain in his stomach.

Realizing that he was about to die and unable to delude himself with false hopes, he decided to say good-bye to his nearest friends. He therefore went into Dashenka's bed-room, for he was a widower and Dashenka, an old maid, was keeping house for him.

"Dashenka," he said with a sob, "dear Dashenka!"

Something stirred in the dark and emitted a deep sigh.

"Dashenka!"

"Who is it?" said Dashenka with a start. "Oh, is it you, Pyotr Petrovitch? Are you back already? Well? Did they name the baby? Who was the god-mother?"

"Natalya Andreyevna was the godmother, and Pavel Ivanitch was the god-father, and I think I am dying, Dashenka. The baby was named Olympiada. . . and. . . I have drunk kerosene."

"What! You don't mean to say they gave you kerosene, do you?"

"I'll make a clean breast of it. I wanted to take a little nip of whiskey without getting your permission. . . and. . . God punished me for it. By mistake I took kerosene in the dark. . . What shall I do now?''

When she heard that her cupboard had been opened without her permission she jumped to her feet. Hastily lighting a candle, she drew herself to her full angular and bony height, and forgetting to throw anything over her nightgown she shuffled in her bare feet over to the cupboard.

''Who gave you permission?'' she cried, opening the cupboard. ''Nobody ever put the whiskey there for your benefit!''

''I. . . I. . . have drunk kerosene, Dashenka, not whiskey. . .'' mumbled Strizhin, wiping the cold perspiration from his face.

''And why should you be nosing around my kerosene? Is it any of your business? I didn't buy it for you, did I? If you only knew what a devilish price I've had to pay for it! You know nothing about that, of course you don't!''

''Dear Dashenka,'' he groaned, ''it is a question of life and death, and you speak about money!''

''Not satisfied with getting drunk, he comes around sticking his nose into the cupboard!'' raged Dashenka, shutting the door of the cupboard with a bang. ''You bandit, you torturer, you! Not a minute of rest have I! By day and by night you ruin me! Robber, murderer! May you live in the next world as peacefully as you let me live here! Tomorrow I am going to leave this place. I am a virgin and I refuse to let you remain in my presence in your underwear! And don't you dare to look at me when I am undressed!''

She gave loose rein to her tongue and away it galloped, on and on and on. . .

Knowing that nothing could be done with her in her fit of anger, that neither soft words nor harsh, neither prayers nor oaths, nor even bullets would be of any avail, Strizhin made a gesture of despair, dressed himself and went in search of a doctor. But doctors and policemen are found only when not needed. He ran through several streets, rang five times at one doctor's house, seven times at another's, and finally hastened over to the drug store. Perhaps the druggist would help.

After a long pause a little, dark, curly-headed druggist opened the door. He was dressed in his bathrobe and his eyes were still sleepy, but his face inspired a feeling of awe, so stern and intelligent was its expression.

"What can I do for you?" he asked in tones which only smart and worthy druggists know how to employ.

"For God's sake, I beseech you!" cried Strizhin breathlessly. "Give me something, anything! . . I've just drunk kerosene! I'm dying!"

"Now, don't become excited, my good fellow, but answer the questions that I am going to put to you. Your nervous frame of mind makes it impossible for me to understand you. You have drunk kerosene. Am I right?"

"Yes! Kerosene! Save me!"

The druggist solemnly went to his counter, opened a book and was lost in deep meditation. Having perused a couple of pages, he shrugged one shoulder, then the other, made a grimace, mused for a minute or two and then went into a rear room. At this moment the clock struck four. At precisely a quarter to five he returned from the rear room with another book and once more was lost in deep perusal.

"H'm!" he finally said in perplexity. "The very fact that you feel bad shows that you ought to go to a doctor instead of a druggist."

"But I've already been to doctors! I rang and rang, but nobody answered."

"H'm! Evidently you don't regard us druggists as human beings. It's nothing to you to wake us up even at four o'clock at night. Every dog, every cat has its rest. . . But you will not listen to it. You imagine that we are not human, and that our nerves are made of hemp!"

Strizhin listened patiently till the druggist finished his harangue, sighed and went home.

"I guess it is my fate to die!" he thought.

His mouth was as hot as a furnace, his throat was choking with the odor of kerosene, his stomach writhed with cramps and his ears were deafened with a ringing noise: boom! boom! boom! Every moment he thought that he was dying and that his heart would beat no more. .

When he returned home, he quickly penned the following note: "I hold no one responsible for my death." Then he uttered a prayer, stretched himself out on his bed and drew a quilt over his head.

Till sunrise he lay awake waiting for his death and picturing to himself how his grave would be strewn with fresh flowers and how the birds would be singing above him. . .

In the morning he was sitting on his bed and talking to Dashenka:

"Whoever lives a normal and temperate life, my dear friend, is immune from every harm, even poison. Take me, for example; I was already standing with both feet in the grave, I suffered, I died, — and now, lo and behold! I only feel a slight bitter taste in the mouth and my throat is a little burned; but as for my entire body, why, thank God. . . And why? Because I lead a normal and decent life."

"Not at all! This only shows that my kerosene was worthless!" sighed Dashenka, thinking only of the price it cost. "This merely shows that the grocer, instead of giving me his best kerosene, gave me the stuff that costs only a cent and a half a quart! Good God, what robbers those people are! How they will take advantage of a poor, helpless woman! Thieves, murderers! May they live in the next world as peacefully as they let me live here! What blood-suckers they are! . ."

And her tongue gathered more and more steam as it galloped on and on and on.

That "Fresh Kid"

IVAN Ivanitch Lapkin, a young man of pleasant appearance, and Anna Semyonovna Zamblitskaya, a young girl with a snub nose, descended the steep river-bank and sank down upon a bench. The bench was situated close by the water's edge, hidden among thick willow bushes. What a splendid lovers' cove! Here one might sit hidden from all the world, seen only by the fish and the water-spiders, that darted here and there like streaks of lightning. The young couple were provided with fishing-rods, bags, cans of worms and everything else needed for a fishing excursion.

No sooner were they seated than they betook themselves to their work.

"I'm so glad that we're alone at last, began Lapkin after looking around. "I have so much to tell you, Anna Semyonovna .... So much... When I saw you for the first time... You've got a nibble there!... Then, for the first time I understood my life's purpose; then I saw for the first time the goddess to whom I must dedicate my entire life work... It looks as if a big fellow's tugging at your line!... When I beheld you, for the first time I learned to love, to love passionately! Don't pull yet... Let him get a good bite... Tell me, my All, I entreat you—not whether I may hope for my love to be returned, for I am unworthy of such good fortune and must never dream of it—but tell me whether I may ever look forward to... Pull!"

With a scream Anna Semyonovna jerked the hand that held the rod high into the air. A silvergreen perch glistened in the sun.

"Good heavens, a perch! Ah! oh!... Quick! He'll wiggle off!"

The perch worked himself free of the hook, began to flop about on the grass and at length fell with a splash back into its native element.

During the pursuit of the fish Lapkin, altogether unaware of it, had seized instead of the fish, Anna Semyonovna's hand and raised it inadvertently to his lips... The girl, indeed, had withdrawn her hand, but it was already too late; unawares the lips had joined in a kiss. Everything had occurred so totally unawares. The first kiss was succeeded by a second; thereupon followed pledges and vows... Happy moments!

After all, there is upon this earth of ours no such thing as absolute happiness. Every joy either carries its poison within itself, or is poisoned by something from without. So did it prove here. Even while the young folks were kissing there suddenly resounded an explosion of laughter. They looked toward the river and their eyes distended with amazement: there, up to his hips in water, stood a naked boy. It was the school-boy Kolya, Anna Semyonovna's brother. He stood in the water, looked at the young folks and laughed diabolically.

"Ah—ah—ah... So you're kissing?" he taunted. "Fine! I'll tell mamma."

"I hope that you, as a man of honor..." Lapkin began to stammer, blushing, "Eavesdropping is contemptible and gossip is mean, despicable... I hope that you, as a person of breeding and as a man of honor..."

"Give me a rouble and I won't tell!" replied the man of honor. "If you don't, I'll blab!"

Lapkin took a rouble from his pocket and handed it to Kolya, who crumpled the note into his wet fist, whistled and swam off. And they kissed no more that day.

The next day Lapkin brought for Kolya, from the city, a box of paints and a ball; his sister, too, presented him with all her pretty pill-boxes. And after that she had to give him a set of dog's head cuff-buttons.

All this largess was manifestly pleasing to the mischievous rascal, and in order to extort more he began to play the spy. Wherever Lapkin and Anna Semyonovna were, there he was, too. Not for a moment did he let them out of sight.

"The scamp!" exclaimed Lapkin, gnashing his teeth. "So young and already such a dangerous scoundrel! What will become of him later?"

Throughout the entire month of June Kolya gave the poor lovers not a moment's rest. He threatened them with betrayal, spied upon them and extorted all kinds of gifts. His demands became more and more extortionate and finally he began to talk of a gold watch. And what was the result? The gold watch had to be forthcoming.

Once during dinner, just as the waffles were being served, he suddenly burst into laughter, winked to Lapkin with one eye and said, "Shall I tell her? Yes?"

Lapkin turned frightfully red and instead of the waffles began to chew his napkin. Anna Semyonovna sprang up from her seat and ran into the next room.

The young couple suffered in this state of affairs until the end of August,—until the day on which Lapkin finally proposed to Anna Semyonovna. Oh, what a joyous day was that! After Lapkin had spoken to her parents and had received their consent, he dashed into the garden and began to hunt for Kolya. When he had found him he almost choked with rapture and seized the mischievous rascal by the ear. Anna Semyonovna, who had also been on the hunt for Kolya, appeared at this instant and seized his other ear. And it would have done your heart good to behold the delight that shone on the lovers' faces as Kolya cried and begged, "Darling sister! Dearest friend! I won't do it any more... Ow, ow, ow! Forgive me!"

Afterwards they both confessed that during the entire period of their courtship and betrothal they never experienced such happiness, such brimming ecstasy, as during those moments when they were pulling that "fresh kid" by the ears.

Such is Fame!

THE passenger of the first class, who had just finished dinner in the railway station, was a trifle drowsy; he lay down upon the velvet sofa, stretched himself out with a grunt of contentment and was soon dozing.

He lay thus, however, for but five minutes; then he awoke, looked with dreamy eyes at his neighbor, who sat directly opposite him, smiled and said, "My late father, blessed be his memory, was fond of having women scratch his heels after dinner. I take after him, with this one difference, that after dinner I like to scratch my tongue and my head. I, sinner that I am, like to prattle on a full stomach. Will you allow me to prattle a bit with you?"

"With pleasure," answered his neighbor.

"After a good dinner, at the slightest opportunity the deepest thoughts begin to flood my mind. For instance, just now we saw with you, at the lunch-counter, two young men, and you heard one of them congratulating the other because of his popularity. 'I congratulate you,' he said, 'you are already a popular personage, you are beginning to acquire fame.'

"They must be actors or journalists. But it is not they who interest me. What interests me is the question: What should we really understand by the word fame or popularity? What is your opinion? According to Pushkin fame is a bright patch upon a worn-out garment. We all look upon it the same way Pushkin does,—that is, more or less subjectively, but up to the present no one has given a clear, logical definition of the word. I would give much for a concise explanation of the word fame."

"Why does it concern you so deeply?"

"Well, if we knew precisely what fame was, you understand,

46

then perhaps we should know also how to attain it," answered the passenger of the first class after brief meditation. "I must tell you, sir, that when I was younger, I strained every string of my soul in the quest of fame. In the first place, I am an engineer by profession. I've built a score of wonderful bridges in various parts of Russia, installed water systems in three cities, have worked in Russia, England, Belgium... In the second place, I've written a large number of special treatises on matters connected with my profession. Thirdly, my good sir, from earliest childhood I've had a weakness for Chemistry; devoting my leisure time to that science I discovered means of extracting many organic acids, for which reason you can meet my name in all foreign study books on Chemistry. I'll not burden you with an account of all my services and accomplishments,—I shall merely tell you that I accomplished far more than many celebrities. And the result? As you see, I am already old and ready to die, and I'm just as much known as that black dog running across the tracks over there."

"How do you know? Perhaps you *are* famous?"

"H'm! We'll soon see... Tell me, did you ever hear of the Krikunov family?"

The other man raised his eyes to the ceiling, thought a while and began to laugh.

"No. Can't say that I have..." he replied.

"That's my family. You are an elderly, educated person, and you never heard of me.—Isn't that sufficient proof? I guess, in my chase after fame, striving to become known, popular, I didn't do as I should have done. I didn't employ the proper means and, wishing to catch fame by the tail, I didn't approach it from the right direction..."

"What proper means do you refer to?"

"Devil knows! You will say... Talent? Genius? Uncommon gifts? That's a mistake, my friend... In my own time people have lived and made reputations who, in comparison with me, are incapable, good-for-nothing and altogether worthless. They did not strive, did not dazzle with their talents, did not pursue fame, yet behold them now! Their names are often mentioned in the papers and in conversation! If you're not already wearied of listening, I'll illustrate my point with an example.

"A few years ago I was constructing a bridge in the city of K... I must tell you that there isn't a deader place in the whole world. If it weren't for the women and cards, I'd have gone out of my mind. Well, that's an old story. Just to kill time I made friends there with a singer. Devil knows, they all used to go wild over her, and in my own opinion—how shall I express it?— she was a most commonplace, average young lady, of a type that is altogther too common, — an empty-headed thing, capricious, envious and a silly goose to boot. She ate a good deal, drank a good deal, slept until five in the afternoon and even later. A mediocre specimen, as you see. She was looked upon as a wanton woman—that was her profession—but when folks wanted to speak of her in literary language they would refer to her as 'the actress,' or 'the singer.' In those days I was a passionate theatre-goer, and I would fly into a rage when I heard her called an actress. She had absolutely no right to the name actress or singer. She was a creature without a spark of talent, without an atom of feeling,—one might say, in sum, a poor little good-for-nothing.

"As far as I understand singing, she sang frightfully,—badly enough to make you faint. Her whole 'art' consisted in her displaying her hosiery, when it was needed, and in letting men into her dressing-room.

"She preferred, naturally, foreign vaudevilles,—spicy ones, with singing and such, in which she could appear in masculine attire. In a word, one of the 'real things!' But just listen to this. I remember it as clearly as if it happend this very day. The bridge was ready to be thrown open to the public. It was opened with solemnity,—prayers, speeches, telegrams and so on.

I myself ran about all flustered, with my child, the work of my brain, and was afraid that my heart would burst with excitement. It was *my* work! It's an old story, and I may permit myself a bit of pride, so let me inform you that the bridge turned out to be a masterpiece! Not a bridge, but a picture, an inspiration! How could I help being excited, when the whole city turned out for the grand opening?

" 'Well,' I thought, 'now the whole public will look at me,— all eyes will seek me. Where can I hide?'

"But, my good sir, my agitation was all in vain. Outside of the official personages nobody even gave me a glance. They gathered at the river bank, staring at the bridge like so many wax figures, without giving so much as a passing thought to him who had created the bridge. And since then, devil take them, I've begun to hate our worthy public. But just listen. Suddenly a commotion arose among the assembled crowd. Faces beamed, people began to elbow their way forward...

" 'Ah! They've noticed me at last!' I thought. But far from it! I see my friend the singer squeezing through the crowd, and at her heels a whole army of loafers. And all eyes were centered upon her, and thousands of lips whispered, 'That's so and so...isn't she charming! Divinely beautiful!'

"At this point I, too, was noticed by a couple of idlers, most likely local lovers of the dramatic art. Seeing me, they scrutinized me and began to murmur, 'That's her lover.'

"How do you like that? A man in a silk hat, and with a jaw that for a long time had not been scraped by a razor, stood near me for quite a while, raising now one foot and now the other, and finally accosted me.

" 'Do you know who that lady is, walking there at the river's edge? That's so and so... Her voice is beneath all criticism, but she certainly knows how to use it!'

" 'Can you tell me?' I asked the man in the silk hat, 'who constructed this bridge?'

" 'Upon my word, I don't know!' replied the silk hat. 'Some engineer or other!'

" 'And who,' I asked, 'built this church for your city?'

" 'I can't tell you that, either.'

"I further asked the silk hat who was considered the leading professor of the city,—the foremost architect,—and to all these queries I received from the silk hat a single reply:

" 'I don't know. Can't tell you.'

" 'Tell me, pray,' I asked at last, 'with whom does this noted singer live?'

" 'With a certain engineer by the name of Krikunov,' replied the silk hat without hesitation.

"Well, how do you like that, my friend?... But listen to the rest of the story... On the day following the christening of the bridge I seized the daily paper to discover something—about myself, about the builder of the bridge. For a long time I scanned all four pages of the paper and finally—found! Hurrah! I begin to read:

> Yesterday, under a smiling sky, in the presence of His Excellency the governor and other government officials, a vast municipal gathering celebrated the opening of the new bridge, etc.

"The news report concluded in this fashion:

> Among others there was also present at the opening our beloved and gifted artist, Miss So and So. As is easily understood, her appearance created a furore. The noted actress was dressed in . . . etc.

"About me,—not a single word, not a syllable! As insignificant as the matter was, in that moment it grieved me so keenly that I burst into tears.

"I soothed myself with the consolation that the province was of mediocre intelligence, incapable of appreciating such a work, and that it was foolish to expect recognition from such people; that it was possible to acquire fame only in intellectual centers, in the metropolitan cities.

"Well, there was at Petersburg at that time one of my works that I had submitted in a competition. The day of the award was drawing nigh.

"I bade farewell to the city of K— I took the train for Petersburg. It's a long distance from K— to Petersburg. In order to drive away lonesomeness I took a separate coupé and also...the singer. We rode along and on the whole way did nothing but eat, guzzle champagne and tra-la-la! Had a great old time!... And at last there we were in Petersburg, in the great intellectual center. I arrived on the very day of the award, and had the pleasure, my dear friend, of celebrating a victory: my work was honored with the first prize. Hurrah!

"The next day I go to Nevski Prospekt and squander all of seventy kopeks on newspapers. I return to my hotel, sink back into the sofa and bury myself in the newspapers, all the while quivering with excitement.

"I look through one paper—nothing! A second—not a word! At length, in the fourth journal I come upon an announcement like this:

> Yesterday there arrived in Petersburg by express the noted artiste of the provinces, Miss So and So. We are delighted to state that the Southern climate has had a very beneficial effect upon our well-known friend. Her splendid artistic appearance. . . .

"I can't recall the rest! At the bottom of the page, under the same news item, printed in the smallest size type, was the following:

> Yesterday, at the award of prizes in the such-and-such competition, the engineer So-and-So received first prize.

"And that was all! And to add insult to injury, they twisted my name about. Instead of Krikunov, they printed Kirkunov. There's your intellectual center! But that was not all...

"A month later, when I had left Petersburg, all the papers were screaming without cease about 'our divine, highly-gifted,' and my lady love was lauded by the public press as if she really amounted to something...

"Several years later I happened to be in Moscow. The head of the Moscow Duma had invited me thither, by personal letter, in regard to a subject in which the entire press of Moscow has been interested for more than a century.

"Among other things I delivered at one of the Museums five public lectures for a public cause. That, I imagine, was sufficient to make a fellow talked about in the city, for three days at least? But, nothing doing! Not a single paper in Moscow had even a word in reference to me! They were full of fires, cheap musical comedies, drunken merchants—of everything under the sun except my affair, my project, my lectures. About these, not a syllable!

"I ride in the electric cars...packed, ladies with officers, students of both sexes—each paired after its own kind.

" 'They say that the Duma invited a certain engineer in regard to such and such a project.' I say to my neighbor in a loud voice, so that all may hear. 'Do you know the engineer's name?'

"The fellow shook his head. No. The rest of the people in the car looked at me, and in all their faces I read, 'I don't know.'

" 'They say that somebody's giving lectures in the so and so Museum,' I continue, addressing another, wishing to start a conversation. 'They say that the lectures are very interesting.'

"Nobody stirred. Evidently not one of them had heard of these lectures, and the woman did not even know that such a museum was in existence. But that is not all. Just imagine, my dear friend. All of a sudden the whole crowd in the car sprang from their places and rushed to the window. What was the matter? What had happened?

" 'Look! Look! my neighbor cried, poking me in the ribs.

'Do you see that dark fellow sitting there in that droshke? That's the famous king of the thugs!'

"And the whole crowd began to talk with great animation about the thugs who at that time interested the brains of Moscow.

"I could adduce numerous examples of the same kind. But I believe these are sufficient.

"Now let me, for the sake of argument, admit that I am mistaken in regard to myself,—that I myself am only a conceited ass without a spark of talent. But I could point out to you a multitude of men, in my own time, who were remarkably gifted as concerns talent and love of their work and yet who died unrecognized. All the Russian sailors, chemists, physicists, mechanics, farmers—who among us knows them? Are our Russian painters, sculptors and authors known to the intellectual masses? Many an old literary dog with genuine talent wears out the thresholds of editorial offices for thirty-three years, writing reams and reams of material, is twenty times sued for libel and yet cannot go a step further than his ant-hill! Tell me the name of a single genius in Russian literature that was known in his own land before he had been recognized all over the world, or had been killed in a duel, or had gone insane, or else had been condemned for life to hard-labor in Siberia,—or else, had acquired a reputation for cheating at cards."

The passenger of the first class had grown so excited that he took his cigar out of his mouth and arose.

"Yes," he continued, still roused to a high pitch, "and in contrast to such persons I'll show you hundreds of insignificant singers, acrobats and other clowns who have been heard of even by infants in the cradle! Yes, sir!"

The door creaked and a gust of wind blew in, and there entered a third person with an angry countenance, wearing a cape, a silk hat and blue spectacles. The newcomer looked at the vacant places, frowned and continued on his way.

"Do you know who that is?" came a timid voice from a

distant corner of the car. "That is N. N., the famous teller, who is being sued by the A... Bank."

"There you have it!" laughed the passenger of the first class. "He knows the teller, all right, yet ask him whether he knows Semiradski, Chaikovski, or the philosopher Solovyov, and he'll shake his thick head!... Rabble!"

A brief silence.

"Allow me to ask you a question," coughed the neighbor opposite him, diffidently. "Is the name Pushkov familiar to you?"

"Pushkov? H'm!... Pushkov... No. I never heard of such a name"

"That's my name..." continued the neighbor, embarrassed. "So you never heard of me? And for thirty-five years I have been professor in one of Russia's leading universities...a member of the Academy of Science... More than once my treatises have been printed..."

The passenger of the first class and his neighbor looked at each other and burst into long and loud laughter.

Overspiced

THE surveyor Smirnov got off at Snoozeville Station. He still had about thirty or forty miles to go before reaching his destination.

"Will you please tell me where I can get some post-horses?" he asked of the ticket agent.

"What's that? Post-horses? You can't get any post-horses or even an old, broken-down truck in a hundred miles... Where are you bound for?"

"General Khokhotov's estate."

"Oh, is that so?" yawned the ticket agent. "Well, in that case you had better go over there to that house behind the station. The fellow that lives there sometimes takes passengers."

With a sigh the surveyor betook himself to the designated place where, after considerable searching and arguing and complaining, he found a sturdy peasant, with an evil pock-marked face, who wore a tattered smock and coarse straw boots.

"The devil knows what sort of a wagon this is!" said the surveyor with a grimace as he clambered into the vehicle. "It's hard to tell which is the front and which is the back..."

" 'Tain't hard to tell at all," replied the peasant. "The front is over there near the horse's tail and the back is over here where Your Honor is sitting."

The colt was young, but lean, knock-kneed and frazzled around the ears.

The driver took his seat and whipped the mare; her only reply was a nod of the head. He swore at her and whipped her again; the wagon creaked and shivered as though it had the ague. He struck a third blow; the wagon began to bob. Finally at the fourth blow the wagon stirred from its place.

"Are we going to drag along like this all the way?" asked the surveyor, who felt that his very life was being rattled out of him although the wagon scarcely moved.

"We'll g-g-get there, all r-right!" the peasant reassured him. "She's a young little mare and she certainly can run once she gets started. You just wait till she gets a-going, and you won't be able to hold your seat...Hey you, giddap, you nasty old nag!"

The wagon left the station at dusk. To the right stretched a dark frozen plain which seemed to extend to the very banqueting halls of the devil. At the horizon, where the wide steppe melted into the sky, the cold faint lights of the setting autumn sun were burning out... To the left, confused hilly shapes loomed up here and there in the twilight. It was hard to tell whether these were haystacks or trees. The surveyor was unable to see in front of him, because the peasant's massive back blotted out the entire landscape. A cold, frosty stillness held the entire region in its grip.

"What a wilderness!" thought the surveyor, putting the collar of his coat over his ears. "No sign of a dwelling and not a living soul in sight. If robbers should attack me, nobody would hear my cries, nobody would even know where to look for my bones... And this driver is not at all to my fancy... Did you ever see such a back? A big husky like him could beat the soul out of the likes of me with one finger! And his snout, too, is strange and angular like a wild beast's."

"Look here, my friend," asked the surveyor. "What's your name?"

"My name? Klim."

"Listen, Klim. Is it quiet in these parts? Is is safe? I mean, are people raising the devil around here?"

"Everything is quiet, thank God... Nobody is raising the devil."

"I am glad to hear nobody is raising the devil... Still!,

I've. . . You never can tell. . . I've taken three pistols along with me," lied the surveyor. . . "And you know very well, my dear fellow, that it is a dangerous thing to play with pistols. With a single revolver I could easily take care of ten robbers. . ."

Night had fallen. The wagon suddenly creaked, began to shake and squeak and then swerved to the left, as if against its will.

"Where is he dragging me?" thought the surveyor. "After going to the right he turns all of a sudden to the left. . . I shouldn't be surprised if he's trying to take me into the woods and. . .God help me!. . .You never can tell. . . Such things do happen!. . .

"Listen!" he turned to the peasant. "You say that there is no danger here?. . . It's really too bad!. . . I love to have a scrap with murderers. . . To look at me, one would take me for a skinny weak-kneed piece of carrion, but by Jove, I've got the strength of an ox. . . . Once I was attacked by three murderers, and what do you think? I gave one of them such a beating that . . . he spit out his soul. . . And the other two were sent away to Siberia for life. . .I don't know, I'm sure, where I've got such strength. . . Why, with one hand I can grab hold of a giant like yourself, for instance, and. . .crumple him up like a piece of paper."

Klim turned around and looked at the surveyor, blinked and whipped up the pony.

"Yes, my good fellow," continued the surveyor, "God pity those who start anything with me. They'll not only lose their arms and legs, but they'll be sent away to Siberia, to boot. . . For every single police judge knows me. . . I am an indispensable person, a cog in the wheel of our government. . . Here I am travelling with you, and the secret service knows all about it. You had better take care that nothing happens to me. . . Everywhere hereabouts, behind every bush policemen and detectives are hidden. . . H-h-hold on!" suddenly cried the surveyor in alarm. "Where are you going? Where are you dragging me?"

"Can't you see? This is a forest."

"Sure enough, it is a forest," thought the surveyor, "and that's just why I am so frightened... But it wouldn't do to show him that I am afraid...He has already noticed how scared I am ... Why in the world does he keep turning around and looking at me? I guess he's already planning how to... At first he was travelling so slowly, but now he's galloping like the very devil!...

"Look here, Klim, what are you hurrying the mare like this for?"

"I'm not hurrying her, she's hurrying of her own accord... Once she gets started, nothing in the world can stop her... Even she herself is sorry for having such hurrying hoofs."

"You're lying, you rascal! I know that you're lying! But just the same I'd advise you to slow her up. Stop her... Do you hear? Stop her!"

"What for?"

"What for? Because I'm expecting four friends from the station... I want them to catch up with me... They promised to overtake me in the forest... It will be more cheerful to travel together with them... They're huskies,—in fact, regular giants, and every mother's son of them has got a pistol... Now what in the world are you looking at me like that for? And why do you bob around as though you were sitting on pins and needles, ha? There's no need of your looking at me. There's nothing extraordinary about my appearance. But my pistols are... really worth looking at! If you want to, I'll take them out and show them to you... Do you want to see them? Hey?"

The surveyor made a motion as if to look for them in his pockets, when he was suddenly amazed to see that which even in his worst fears, he had never expected: Klim rolled off the wagon and on all fours scurried away among the thick bushes.

"Help!" he began to cry. "Help! Take the mare and the wagon and everything, but spare my life! He-elp!"

There was a sound of hurrying footsteps and the crackling of dry branches, and after that all was still... The surveyor, who was dumbfounded at this, stopped the wagon, rearranged the seat under him and began to think.

"He has run away, the fool! What a coward!... But what in the world am I to do now?... I can't go on myself; for, in the first place, I don't know the way, and in the second place, people might suspect me of stealing the mare... What's to be done?"

"Klim!" he called, "Klim!" And the echo rebounded from the forest, "Klim! Klim!"

At the thought that he would have to stay all night in the dark forest where the only sounds were the howling of the wolves and the snorting of the lean mare, the surveyor's terror became almost unbearable.

"My darling little Klim!" he began to cry, "My sweet, dear, darling little Klim! Where are you?"

For about two hours the surveyor continued his entreaties. Finally, when he became hoarse from calling and was already resigned to spend the night in the forest, the breeze brought a faint moan to his ears.

"Is that you, my darling little Klim? Come, let us continue our journey."

"I'm afraid you'll k-k-kill me!" replied a weak voice.

"I was only joking, Klim darling! So help me God, I was only fooling! I have no pistols with me. I only pretended because I was afraid... Have pity on me! Let's go on! I'm frozen!..."

Evidently realizing that a regular robber would long ago have disappeared with the mare, Klim emerged from the bushes and timidly approached his passenger.

"Well, you big jackass, what did you get frightened for? I was only joking and you became scared... Sit down!"

"How should I know, your Honor?" stammered Klim, as he

clambered into the wagon. "If I had only known in the first place, I wouldn't have taken you for a hundred roubles. I almost died of fright..."

Klim whipped the mare; the wagon began to creak and shiver. Klim beat her a second time; the wagon began to bob. Finally at the fourth blow the wagon stirred from its place. The surveyor put the collar of his coat over his ears. His fear was entirely gone.